Mop and the Birthday Picnic

by Martine Schaap and Alex de Wolf

Cricket/McGraw-Hill

"Mop and Family" appears monthly in *Ladybug*® magazine.
Visit our Web site at www.ladybugmag.com or call 1-800-827-0227
or write to *Ladybug* magazine, 315 Fifth Street, Peru, IL 61354.

© 2001 Carus Publishing Company

Printed in the United States of America. Design by Suzanne Beck. All rights reserved. Except as permitted under the United States Copyright Act, no part of this publication may be reproduced or distributed in any form or by any means, or stored in a database retrieval system, without prior written permission from the publisher.

Send all inquiries to:
McGraw-Hill Children's Publishing
8787 Orion Place
Columbus, OH 43240-4027

1-57768-882-1

1 2 3 4 5 6 7 8 9 10 RRD-W 05 04 03 02 01

Library of Congress Cataloging-in-Publication Data

Schaap, Martine.
    Mop and the birthday picnic / by Martine Schaap and Alex de Wolf.
        p. cm.
    Summary: On their birthday, their parents plan surprises for twins Justin and Julie, including special presents and a birthday picnic with their dog Mop. Presents suggestions for picnic recipes and games.
        ISBN 1-57768-882-1
        [1. Birthdays--Fiction. 2. Picnicking--Fiction. 3. Twins--Fiction.]
    I. Wolf, Alex de, ill. II. Title.
        PZ7.S32775 Mh 2000
        [E]--dc21
                                    00-011329

9 781577 688822

"Justin, are you awake?" Julie asked from the bottom bunk.

"Yes . . ." her twin brother answered sleepily.

They were both quiet for a moment, then they shouted "Happy Birthday!" to each other.

Mom and Dad came in singing "Happy Birthday."

1

"Let's have cake for breakfast!" Julie exclaimed.

"And where are our presents?" asked Justin.

"This is a surprise birthday," Dad explained. "The cake comes later."

"Your presents are too big to wrap," Mom added.

"Wow, too big to wrap!" Justin shouted.

"Come on, let's look for them right now," Julie called, running out of the room.

Mop followed the twins to help them search.

First they peeked into the living room. It was beautifully decorated with paper chains, but there were no presents to be seen.

The kitchen was quite empty. No cake on the counter,
and not a single present in sight.

Mop wanted to go outside. "I'll open the door for you,"
said Justin. Suddenly he whooped, "Julie, come and look!"

"Wow . . ." Justin cried.

"Great bikes!" shouted Julie.

"No baby bikes for us anymore. This is just what we needed," Justin explained to Mop.

"New helmets, guys," said Dad. "To go with new bikes."
"Let's go for a ride!" Justin shouted.
"Let's get dressed and have breakfast first," said Mom.
"Then we'll have the next part of the surprise."

7

After breakfast, the twins tried out their bikes while
Mom and Dad packed a picnic basket and a cooler.
"Here we go," said Dad.
"Where are we going?" asked Julie.
"That's a surprise," Mom answered.

It was great weather for a birthday—and for a bicycle ride. Mop enjoyed running along, and the twins enjoyed their speedy new bikes.

"I see water! Look over there!" Julie pointed ahead.

"It's the lake where we went swimming last summer," Justin said.

When they stopped at the lakeside for a break, Mom cycled ahead.

"Wait for us!" Justin shouted after her.
"Let her go, we'll catch up with Mom later," said Dad.
"Look at that duck diving," Julie said.
"That's how it catches its food," Dad explained.

Justin discovered a huge bird, wading through the shallow water and eyeing the water surface. "That heron is looking for food, too, Dad," he said. Quick as lightning the heron snatched a fish out of the water and flew away.

"He takes his prey to a quiet spot to eat it in peace," Dad explained. "Herons like to eat fish and frogs."

"Frogs . . . yuck!" Julie didn't like that idea at all.

Mop spotted a frog sitting on a stone in front of him.

Wanting a closer look, Mop jumped into the water.
But the frog was quicker and took a giant leap. *Croak!*

"Your prey got away, Mop," Julie said, smiling.

"Silly dog, now you're soaked, and you got me wet, too," Justin added.

Soon they were cycling along the lake again. "Now we are going to look for food, just like the animals," Dad said. "Let's catch up with Mom."

"Yes, I'm ready for lunch," Julie said.

"Cycling makes me very hungry!" Justin agreed.

17

"Where can Mom be?" Julie asked.

"Look, Julie!" Justin discovered a chain of flags.

"Next surprise!" Mom's voice called. "It's our picnic!"

"A perfect spot," Dad said. "No bears, no ants—our food will be safe here."

While their parents set the table, the twins started a game of catch.

"Come on, Mop, join us!" they shouted. "Running will dry your coat."

But Mop smelled something good. . . . And he spotted
something that was much more interesting than a frog or
a game of catch—hot dogs!

Mom and Dad joined the last part of the game. Dad
threw toward Justin. "Catch it!" he called.
Justin jumped in the air, but he missed.

Everyone was busy searching in the brush, and this suited Mop just fine....

While nobody was watching, Mop sneaked away,
looking for a quiet spot to enjoy his prey.

Hungry from all the bicycling and playing, the twins sat down at the picnic table. Mom unpacked the food and exclaimed in surprise, "The hot dogs are gone!"

"No bears . . ." Justin said.

"No ants . . ." Julie added.

"But we do have . . . MOP!" they shouted together.

Mop, hearing his name, came running toward the table, holding an empty container.

"I see you've had your feast already," Mom said. "It's a good thing we have a lot of sandwiches, too!"

"I'm glad Mop didn't find our last surprise," Dad said, as he took a cake out of the cooler.

"Great!" Justin shouted.

"The best dessert ever," Julie added. "Surprise birthdays are the best!"

WOOF! Mop agreed.

Picnic Party Ideas

Easy-to-Make Outdoor Treats

Banana Bun

Open a hot dog bun. Spread peanut butter on one side and jelly on the other. Peel a banana and brush it with lemon juice. Put the banana in the bun instead of a hot dog!

Johnny Appleseed's Beans

Ask an adult to help cut the center from several large apples and scoop out all the seeds, leaving a firm shell. Mix one tablespoon of orange marmalade into one can of baked beans. Fill the apples with the bean mixture and wrap them in heavy-duty foil. Ask the adult to place the packages on medium-hot coals for about 30 minutes, or until the apples feel tender. Eat with a spoon, right from their skins!

Rolled Sandwiches

Use a rolling pin to flatten a slice of whole-wheat bread. Spread with your favorite sandwich topping, such as peanut butter, flavored cream cheese, or cheese spread. Roll up the bread with the topping on the inside.

Dangling Dessert

Tie strings to doughnuts and hang them in a row from a low tree branch. Have friends or family line up, one person to each doughnut. Try to eat the doughnuts without using any hands!

Fun and Games

Juggle Ball

In advance, gather empty one-gallon milk jugs, one for each person. Wash the jugs and ask an adult to help you cut two inches off the bottom of each one. Put masking tape over the cut edge so it isn't rough or sharp.

To play: hold the jug, cut side up, by the handle and use it to toss a ball or beanbag back and forth. If the ball falls on the ground, simply scoop it up with the jug and keep playing. How long can you keep the ball in the air?

29

Puppy, Chase Your Tail

All the players stand in a line, holding the person in front of them around the waist. Tuck a bandanna into the waistband of the last person in line. The first person in line tries to capture the bandanna "tail," while those at the back of the line try to keep it out of reach.

How long can the "puppy" chase its tail without breaking the chain of people? When the puppy catches its tail, the game starts over with a different person in front and a different person in back.

Twosome Tag

All but two players join up in pairs. They spread out around the playing area and link elbows, two by two. Each pair stays in one spot. The two players who are not linked begin playing "tag" around the pairs of players. But the person being chased can escape by linking elbows with someone in one of the pairs. When this happens, the person on the other side of that pair has to let go and becomes the person being chased.